D1499996

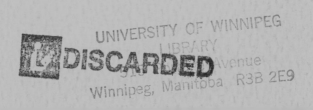

UNIVERSITY OF WINNIPEG
LIBRARY
Avenue
Winnipeg, Manitoba R3B 2E9

DISCARDED

THE PAGE-TURNER

ALSO BY DAVID SHAPIRO

January
Poems from Deal
A Man Holding an Acoustic Panel

Co editor: *An Anthology of New York Poets*

PS
3569
H34P3

THE
PAGE-TURNER

DAVID SHAPIRO

 LIVERIGHT : New York

To my parents

Copyright © 1972, 1973 by David Shapiro
All rights reserved. No part of this book may
be reproduced in any form without permission
in writing from the publisher.

The author gratefully acknowledges the editors
of the following journals, in which certain of the poems
in this book first appeared:
The New Yorker, Partisan Review, Poetry (Chicago),
Sun, World.

1.98765431

ISBN: 87140-575-X
Library of Congress Catalog Number: 73-82427

Designed by Mary M. Ahern
Manufactured in the United States of America

CONTENTS

THE PAGE-TURNER

THE PAGE-TURNER

"Perhaps we can imagine a book like this one. . . ."
—Clive Kilmister, *The Nature of the Universe*

The cover of the book is itself exactly
Page one is you within a small room
Page three already a fair field for your tomb
Page four contains Newark matter-of-factly

Page five appropriates all its frightening streets
On page six Greater Manhattan glumly fits
There is room on page seven for all deceits
And on page eight the earth comfortably sits

And now the pages get much more inspiring
We turn again and not much can be seen
Though on page ten the moon begins soaring
Into details, darkness comes in on page eleven

On page twelve we see bodies not unlike
Our body, let's leave them at this stage
Now we can see the sun the first star for our sake
That moved us from the center of our page

Like us the asteroids are always travelling
And other rocky lumps that never waver
And now miles are an inconvenient thing
The traveller ages less than the observer

That solar system has withered to a dot
And we've been turning pages for light years
By twenty-two your naked eye is shot
By all the naked stars when night was yours

Naked-eyed page-turners around the world,
Turn very rapidly to page twenty-three
Two dinner plates is our galaxy
Vague whiteness in which the main course is still veiled

Let's turn one more page, page twenty-five
Now we are the cluster known as Local Group
Moving hither and thither as if alive
And we are, some stars, others merely hot soup

On page twenty-seven we approach the limit
And we are neither unique nor rare
No matter how far we go into it
At the end of our amazement is distant air

Now we really seem to be near the end
Covering one more page at enormous speeds
And what can we expect, from our imaginary hand
On page twenty-eight, when all we see recedes?

THE MUSIC STAND

On the music-stand the music stands like softened skin.
And outside the peony, burning with silent thirst.
You in rayon with your ton of discs frisk in the garden
Playing an artificial Eskimo basketball with leaves that rust.

There is no saucer of love for the peony,
Only a little brutal water from pipes.
The sink was on fire, death to all leaves, Mother sleepy,
As Autumn flagged or breezed out near the pumps.

Come and go, my numina, ransack the music!
You were found unwilling to be snapped
With Her, hovering over such depths as bees among their own
                claque
As Judy danced behind the grillework.

With "your name on their stingers" they couldn't catch you
Apparently advancing to your own room
Slowly whirling the black Lazy Susan (you loved your own
                games)
Before malaise lit your head with an emotionless beam.

Then the ball would smash in, as if to prove perspective!
And the bell, and time to quit gym for orchestra
Wondering what your seat would be in the orchestra of heaven.
Oh my pianist, let me sit beside you as a page-turner!

You said, "The violinist does not like his repertoire tonight.
The pianist looks at the rented stool with some pain.
The page-turner, from Russia, faces his task with delight
And hopes he will be called to serve thus again.

"The violinist knows that the rehearsals before
Were too short; the pianist looks at the little shore
Of white keys and feels a most divided will.
The page-turner is at his highest peak still.

"The violinist lifts his violin, as if in a high wind.
The pianist also has treachery in mind
Placing one finger on the white part.
The page-turner is silent, in the best tradition of his art.

"A dinosaur attacks, only to be attacked in the back by a Rex
            and crushed
It is tragic for a girl to love in an attic
Filled with such plaster-of-paris, a warehouse of castaways
If noble, decomposing in the weather, where the maids have
            washed."
            .

On the music-stand the music stands like softened skin.
The shuffling has stopped. I walk the plank.
I used to be a blank. And now I am a blank.
Oh my pianist, let me sit beside you as a page-turner!

THE NIGHT SKY

To look up in your face
Is like looking into the devastated night sky
Lights of all kinds I trace
Animals, battles, the whole picture rotating by

Now the nervous system is suspended
Your total mass enjoys recuperation
In repose our theories are almost ended
You are inert as Eve in hibernation

The sailors go to sleep, and then their sails
And then a dead ocean falls upon my mind
I think of grapes put to sleep or apples
Kind apples and night's welcome officer wind

Let us return now to your hair
So long and inconvenient
Fixed to you and waving like that slowly rotating star
Swept past one's vision to make a point

Sharp flashes of those eyes show you once a week
So well within the behavior which is yours
Deliberately trying to find someone else in the universe awake
Life, a long way ahead of ours

Your body is no bigger than the earth
Dreaming outside the sudden switch of the sun
Sending off attached clouds as little worth
And twinkling your closed eyes: their work is done

But not your lips triumphantly open
Musically since the ear is ready
Weightless as a knife in air will sharpen
And the billiard ball grow giddy

I would thread with a hook and eye your dress
Fasten you to me with a rod or bolt
Pass through like a curtain rod your eyes
And they never shut

You are relative to the distant stars
Not smeared out to a lump, a leaf
A lot of annihilation is going on, you cut your hairs
But the hair grows back and not the knife

We are fixed at both ends forever
In the frequency of the fundamental cave
Holding us is a musician however
Like a string and like a wave

THE TORCHES OF THE BACCHAE

Cold light,
still living,
by the light
of this rotten fruit
and by the light
of the luminous mutton of Montpellier,
juicy and in good condition,
placed in a dark room
like the belly of an earthworm,
stones you handed me
yes, but luminous human beings?
though these are occasions
to be the firefly
not the spider,
the firefly with its "will to flash"
delayed, trapped
and behaving itself
while the Bacchae
with fatuous lamps
bring milk out of the Tiber
Dusty hair I'll rub again
again against the grain, though
a gland gets filled with bacteria
and squeezed into that sea of
recorded river shrimp
and retarded beach fleas

Perpetual lamps
And I have observed the
light of small worms
stimulated by moving
over such burbling outlines,
outlining the body with cat's eyes
that makes you famous a while
eventually killing you
when excited, far from "in vacuo"
when the crabs are difficult
around your waist
and below: brittle stars
and snake stars
are the occasion of the silent discharge
striking your by now helpless eyes
Brilliant points stuck
to my handkerchief then,
the waves broke around me
like a tissue,
I had the satisfaction
of seeing Figure 46,
filled with luminous specks,
and the light since escaped me,
and my fingers touched it,
and even the bile
was a faint source of light
placed as we are in the
great bucket,
but very rapidly receding
along its veil and crest

Your cat at Deal was rubbing
fur along the tip of the church
steeple as you removed your blouse
A star began to settle

and we had theories of auroras
but stuck to ourselves,
not hurting, but rather
gently licking with fire
Frisking about dead thistles
I never saw glowworms in such numbers,
and fireflies emitting splendor,
and as they recede
others approached at top speed
"*Ignis fatuus* . . . bewitches
leads men into pools and ditches"
Fetch me the light,
kitty with a wisp,
no light at all, but a
classic wisp, nonetheless
your almost human hair
professor of linen,
shining in the night (of 1990–1?)
a detail for terror: no heat,
no smoke, no good or bad
and the blouse was not burnt
And we went walking
in the rotten wood

And after much walking
removed those clothes
whose sweat was luminous
and saw those wounds
by the baffling light of blood
As soldiers began to prepare
potato soup
and discard potatoes
in the President's pail
As darkness falls
the same potatoes give off charcoal light

a light by which it's possible
to read, in characters of print
"*Si je ne m'abuse pas*
ce fait est très singulier
et merite quelque attention
de la part des physiciens"
placed as we are in the great bucket,
but veering rapidly
along its veil and crest,
to dissect for the lantern of the firefly,
I place you on the table ,and it scatters into light.

FREMITUS

1.

If everyone is listening and no-one is sending
Then posterity alone will take advantage
Of the organized soup of common events and pictures.
Now for the first time we saw the inflammable rivers.

The game, in this respect, was just beginning:
Playing with a hypothetical team an unintelligible game
Over the hope for a less beleagured board as the players
Move forward with the irresistible message of a cricket.

It may have happened only once,
Music which is certainly the essential prelude,
Towers and farms unable to predict how often they swarm
Arising from far-fetched beds with our familiars,

Capable of only the most limited of love,
And using these pulsing organs to advance,
The pulses we receive remain suspicious
Like the hazardous decisions of a night after which we will
        see quite differently.

Every bulb, every star that is near us
We carefully monitor and from every black hole near them,
Automated messengers we are carrying flares and pictures
Of men trying to attract the attention of a woman.

There are no clues to look for in the sky,
No obvious radio on which to listen.
Landmarks have become as numerous as the raindrops
That fall on no narrow and therefore logical street.

And, furthermore, what if no-one is listening
And powerfully the others have defected
In an absence of exchange with after all absconded millions
Of years after which blatant conferences were not enriched.

But the children who receive this answer
And who re-established nightly contact in the most economical
            way
Launched the dogs carried upstream by strong tides
Handed to the frightened and friendly waiting at the pier.

This, then, was a guess and a discussion
And in general a rejection
Of firing bombs into the critical atmosphere
As the shepherd managed to rescue the dog.

We were wearing a chain leash and a heavy iron collar
Black and tan and pulled into the tide
Whilst the others crawled in great numbers along similar lines
And the rain froze on snowy Mt. Ararat.

2. In End

"Je voudrais être loin de moi"

—*Reverdy*

I wanted to be sure to get away from my dropping presence
And to reproach the pelican who held those silken drops of ink
Against the giraffe for surcease where all that is has no venue
And all that latent shadow approaches, approaches.

At the center of this indecisive beach is a junketing nature
Where women are dead leaves each turbulence leaves hardened
Then the wind comes to boil them all up by their rainy doors
And on a light couch they become brilliant fainters again.

Oh life on earth is having to face it through fingers
Or little horses where the rider sleeps, smoldering,
Thus panic is a kind of blue drop by drop when you think
And I more thirsty than alive, more reawakened than thinking
        of it.

An incontinent profile I am of the bravura thread which
        somersaults
The horizon also is a thread, precursor of the vaults of shoulders
Where my dessicated hands held a note, a bloody crocus fumed
And all above the invigorated gulf the air walks on down its
        own road.

I also walk because of the clamor of these pistils in the park
And sarcastic reeds pointed out to where the lake lay,
        uninfluential, dead,
Where a hardened frog slept, smoldering,
And unexerted dragon-flies came floating along.

There was a wet blanket of poppies and opium.

We smoothed it down and prepared to romp through the
        honeysuckles,
Night which wrinkled your dress among branches, a branch of
        the tree of sleep,
Night patiently turning our sparklers to cinders.

Having to love, fatigued by syrup, craning your neck after blood,
You enjoyed that detonated rush of peace.
Waking up with aplomb it was not a field but the charnel house
Which you tried to size up in your rayon slip of chiaroscuro.

Sparkles of its old decapitated gold were setting
On all that limestone, but the butterfly larva had evaporated.
"That badly designed window opened on heaven"
The innocuous wound of which I was the victor.

The dog emerged on the horizon, behind my father like a
        life-guard.
His dog's head creating dunes in the sea as he paddled.
The algae beneath us was grey but in a sense more clear than
        words.
My pea-pod sailed on delicately denuded.

Each morning I pretended to put a penny in my tower.
Lame in the evening my mother would catch the reflections
Of Father crawling beyond the poles of the life-guards
Across the clear chest of the sea which like a rat descended.

3.

You see you have carefully amassed a Stradivarius
Of sorts out of all the real Stradivarii

16

That have passed into your repairing hands
Giving the mutilated originals back to their owners.

When I buy a souvenir pencil
And it has a female's private parts
When I hold it up to the light
Those are your parts

"Do not mirror
This is my last poem
I give it to you
I may not be able to finish it this time"

The heart asks pleasure first
And then for seconds
And then excuse from pain
And then those little anodynes

I ask my father
why my heart is beating twice
for every beat it should
He puts his hand upon my chest and says, It's nothing

But your heart is shedding blood
to repair itself
The hypochondriac
is a hidden nurse

My wife has similar symptoms
Jasper Johns makes echo chambers
We are all child prodigies, in a sense
Kenneth is taking a telephone apart, "ambitiously"

A bird with iron beak sits on my hand
I worry and ask my mother will it blind me
I pick up the bird
It does not blind me, but . . .

All that is—is it the intestines of sheep, lambs and goats
Music but a small chain of trills
Made of a chestnut of ivory, shaped like a spoon
A little trumpet, a little adagio,
Plucked by uncontrolled fingers, yielding but one tone?

You were holding loose sheets of music
When I followed you into the store for "The Roots of Harmony"
By this means without any technical knowledge of music
I became familiar with its chief masterpieces, playing them
            myself.

4. THE NEW PARTICLES

In exchange for a little decay
in such a way, for example,
as a positron will combine with an electron,
that is, they will be annihilated,

The little birds decayed also in minutes,
whose flight ended always at the feeding-station
And the bubbles with what surprise is available
abruptly interact with the air
only to form an annihilation star
This was our way—
It continued on, out of the field of view.

1 8

When the clouds lined up in little groups
we children on the jungle gym would separate them
so that their lower parts began to think of gleaming
and underneath the shady day seeped through.
Those days merge, or even hinge, with the same you
but here very close. Why very close? This delicate light
is disturbing as the neighboring knife eliminates it.
The finer the knife, the quicker the boundaries vanish.
"And we do not see where sky ends and the clouds begin
With such clouds and with the sun at our backs."

THE MORE THAN SLOW

Musicians had not strayed long from the serious gray music
       stand
the sky congratulated you for practising, and practising slowly
after years of an impossible desuetude, as in a cast
In dreams you returned the thanks and apologized to the water
       tower
for a little rusty water
In Goethe's day there were no bicycles
so everyone stayed in one place
on the one hand, the men; on the other, the tanned hands
of the gods on the white shoulders of the men
The Kingdom of Heaven was within you but the inside-
outside experience truly frightening as the bees shrugged
the nightmarish scent somehow all that radiance converted into
       wormwood
despite your Viennese élan in the Barbados, hot and aimless
a chuckle in bronze should be your true memorial, more and more
       slowly
in the evening you polished the scratches of the piano with
       shoe-polish
and you turned on the bed like a piano tuner
You lost your confidence in the ambulance
The wings not the firefly in the bottle flew from end to end

LIFE WITHOUT MIND

In ancient Greece and Rome, the system of brain and nerves
was compared to the reservoirs, aqueducts, fountains,
baths, and sewers of that age.

—Leonard A. Stevens, *Explorers of the Brain*

The brain in Greece was once a fountain
In Rome it was an aqueduct of fog
Later it switched into a white telephone
But America is but an analogue

Unrepairable, irreplaceable brain
We have lost our will and way
Mutilations cause no pain
Though we erase the child, destroy the day

The beating heart is lifted from the chest
And placed still beating in another's breast
But you we cannot reinstate by stealth
We have the definition of our death

Out of you the laughs arise
Like a colorful summary
And thinking tears come from your eyes
Like joined hands they fall simultaneously

The rod passed completely through his head
But a man sits up to touch the wound
Astonished physicians order us to bed
Soft-spoken nature gives way to sound

Lightning has incinerated the old frog
And as for the young and healthy dog
He only totters like the zig-zag stars at night
When wishing to turn left he must turn right

And suddenly fall down upon himself
Small skull blown away by a small war
The surface of his thoughts lies on the shelf
Receives the tiny shocks no more

And love's arms thrown out, her fingers extended,
And the needles so callow
The neck on which it all depended
Forces her blonde head back on the pillow

The brain lies above, the maze leads to and from
The brainless beast stands up to say:
"The foot treads upon the thorn, and is dumb,
But the other legs limp away"

The only light in the laboratory
Passes before us like a burning rivet
With a finger a friend approaches our eye
We must not close it

THE CURES OF LOVE

If it rains on Easter Sunday,
It will rain on every Sunday.
I placed a magnet on your body, a spider web across your
          wound,
I took your lady's slippers and drank rock candy with my tea.

You turned your shoes upside down and went to bed early.
I rubbed wild touch-me-nots over the area,
And you loosened up and breathed deeply.
I drilled a hole in a tree, I put your hair in the hole.

You beat me to a powder.
You smeared my brow with crushed onions
You bound wilted beet leaves around my violin
And tied a flour sack around my head.

You placed a nickel under my nose,
Placed scissors, points up, on my neck.
I lay down and put a dime on your heart,
Placed scissors, points up, on your neck.

FOUR SONGS

1.

Oh give that part of blemished Fool
To me, I've burnt the dream without a door
Mine to spiel stories of satin to you
Sleep!   will you be an ocean?

We'll play the mime of sailors and robbers
At the ship's stern sags the hot treasure
And then I'll die upon the shore
Sleep!   oh will you be an ocean?

The die is cast, but foolishly
Heaven's a lot, but hour by hour
All the clocks are iridescent
Sleep?   or were you willing the ocean?

Those same irritating clocks
Will wake us nursing on nominal froth
And banish me from your cool water
Sleep!   oh will you be the ocean?

Ban me like a diesel from the tracks
But give me dreams with half a door
Now your pillow is the floor
Sleep!   while you become the ocean!

2. PRINCESS SUMMER FALL WINTER SPRING

She wears the bathing suit her forefathers wore
And cries to win so much and sheds her fear
As cheers the violin and sheds her white brassiere
Made up for the occasion by Miss Brazil:
The eating stopped but what had been digested tasted ill.

And soon the comets fly, the stars with hair,
Miss Universe walks sadly by forebearing
She has known some time her boyfriend was not there
The single hand of applause was not from him
Among the songs of the air-conditioner
And the radiator after a specious summer interval.

Practically capitulating on stage
The ancient tribunes tell her what to undo
I am undone, cries Princess Summer Fall Winter Spring
The worlds above cry out to be kissed,
And my red lips would kiss them to be tried
If not for the evening gown contest which purses them.

This my answer is original:
I could not hear the answers of other girls
locked as I was in my big glass tent and naturally non-verbal.
And so she walks, and feathers fall, and little cameramen
        converge,
And evening swims off but wrinkling in that light
The bathing suit she wears her mother wore
But the ears of the violin are hers alone,
Whistles from the pedestrian, honks from the double-parked.

She is happy in her way of life, Miss Universe,
Though fired from the phantom mental hospital
Months before it was constructed.
Like a general reclaiming power in the Sudan,
She is in complete control.
And as a plane re-routes toward the enemy, so she, and I
Looked toward the stars with agape, as the burgeoning stage
       left off.

3. THE FAMILY BEAR

If I were a glass polisher and dying of cancer
And you were the registrar of the will
You could cut out my bedroom plate
And file at city hall for the whole estate
And you were a poor belly-dancer

It was a terrible tragedy
And I am responsible
It was my daughter my bear and my land
And I can't blame the child on the one hand
Or the animal

4. THE NIGHT NIGHTS

    This day, the bow-tie of the sun
    This dew, created by bow-ties
    These boats, parading like warts

The world in general loses color
   But the rouge comes and goes, in air
And some brains are scarlet, others gold.

   At the bottom of this big mirror
   Mother Nature plaits her hair
   For all to see—waves, flames, the neighbors
Tracking light down to its brown source in the orient
   And salamanders move
Bathing their grimy pleasures in the jeers of the sea.

   An illustrious moth dresses up
   As a moth whose carcase was dropped by a flame
   And a little wave steps down in froth
Believing its day has come home on the hands of the boats
   The orange ovaries of the shrimp are spilt
In our own Hemisphere we feel nourished by this morsel of
         clarity at last.

   The sun says Get out of my house
   The horizon comes out of it
   And grossly the dew adores it
The torches of the Bacchae are steeped in fatuous fire
   The dawn puts you in your place
Crowning your forehead with some of the fists of love.

   Wealthy and still wondering Night
   Has neither a mouth nor a noise
   For the children on parole
But sits in a reverie in her wasted universe
   As she tries to vote in secret
The wings of the firefly in the bottle fly from end to end.

LITTLE SERVANT
from Max Jacob

I don't like to hear thunder,
I don't want to be burnt by chance,
But if it's by design, Sir,
Blessed be accidents.
But if it's the devil I fear
Let it quickly disappear.

Save me from plague and lepers unattended
Save me from tumors and cancer
But if it's for my contrition you send it
Let it be, thanks, Sir,
And if it's the devil coming near
Make it gallop out of here.

Goitre, goitre, leave your bag
Leave my neck and leave my head
Saint Elmo's fire, Saint-Guy's rag—
If the devil allowed it here
God get it out of here

Let me grow up quickly
and give me a good wife
who won't drink too much whiskey
and beat me the rest of my life

THE ORGAN
from Charles Cros

Long ago when kings were German
Gottlieb died, a musician.
>They nailed him under the organ benches.
>>Hoo!   Hoo!   Hoo!
>The wind blows through the branches.

He died for having loved to his dismay
The little Rose-of-May.
>Girls aren't very honest.
>>Hoo!   Hoo!   Hoo!
>The wind blows through the branches.

She was married one day
To somebody else, lovelessly.
>"Iron the white dresses!"
>>Hoo!   Hoo!   Hoo!
>The wind blows through the branches.

But when they came to church
Gottlieb was no longer at his perch
>As on all other Sundays.
>>Hoo!   Hoo!   Hoo!
> The wind blows through the branches.

But since then, at black midnight,
You can see something twinkle
>At the time of the blue periwinkle.
>>Hoo!   Hoo!   Hoo!
>The wind blows through the branches.

His organ now has pines for pipes.
It makes the little birds keyed-up.
      The heart-broken have their revenges.
            Hoo!   Hoo!   Hoo!
      The wind blows through the branches.

THE MUDGUARD STROKE

"Un nuage passe trop bas"

—Reverdy

Perfect bliss (atomised) like a milk drop
builds a bridge over the valley—too low
or below the belt—
The flood of tears like lashing wine grovels by
                    and is gone
Under the scaffold bedstead of engraved beech
                  where night gets off the subject
Barbed wire, trials and tribulations, blackberry and ivy
The sun hooked up
In creases and dog-ears and undulations
from a breast-high sound barrier of stone
Oh woman in my doorway, in the Straits of Dover
    with your seven-league boots and key money
              crawling on apace with a
              faithful number
The roar of a cannon, the zip of a ball comes
and the mudguard passes
The toot is repeated in this ornamental fountain
The skin of man—nothing but skin and bones-trembles,
rattles like a window, flickers like a light,
falters like a voice, shakes like a hand,
shudders like a whole building
And the ice-cream is shattering the echo
It's a bird taking a walk
It's a bird on the doorstep

a cage bird sticking out of prison
a bird rising from the ranks
It's a bird from a good family discharged from the hospital
          of the branches flying off the handle
A hand which heaves and hoists
the voice that bumps quacks and gobbles
                    And the intelligence dreams

FROM THE NORTH SEA

Dad, you would love to walk
here. Miles of fields
filled with gorse (yellow)
and lupens (lighter yellow).
    Brick cutting
and blackberry bushes nearby.
The younger boys go in
for horse racing and
sailing for speed.
It's cool and windy (50–60F)
though the sun is bright.
You might go mud-skating on
fossiliferous ledges of
the River Alde. You
would love the music here, also.

TWO-FOUR TIME

"L'étoile descend du plafond"

—Reverdy

All of Balzac shines
And your lovely dress twinkles like greedy flares
Evidently my whole heart is conspicuous also in absence
And all of Rome is glimmering through the evening
Fashionable Paris on all sides is glimmering like bugs on water
And all of us were glinting like acacias

Your Persian blinds were made of iron once
In the form of a crossword puzzle
The iron rails off your combustion furnace I guess

One sinks abruptly into the sidestreet
like a glass of water that is on everybody's lips
to wash the wine down
but the trunk isn't down from the attic yet as you hurl yourself
toward that lashing populace all alighting from their puzzles
on the main thoroughfare as the barometer too slopes gently
              down

The violinist goes down his scales
The bell-boy spirals down the stair
The doctor drops the organ rapidly

It is always the same smattering of physics
that one hears singing

34

hinting in a war of quoits that you propose to do nothing
in the matter except float nasty reports
It is always the same word-for-word translation
difficult words like female figures in fresh water
indifferently ceding themselves to blessed positions
provoking pruned editions in the library
like a miscreant functionary pretending to faint
or a list of jewels—enervated female figures
soft in general like nautical light

We don't have the time to say goodbye to the present
Stalling tactics were for the days of Caesar
There isn't the time to say penal servitude or Father Time
                    or stage, phase, step
There isn't time to say sky-blue for that matter
                    or to rest a while

In my youth I washed my hands and came down to dinner
          Down to my mother and father at the proper time
It was like double, triple, or common time
Sky blue the old days now the weather is rotten for months
And one holds out one's hand in a flat trajectory
for a defender but adjoining hands seem also famished
or stringy on the clothes-line bent into a trend
And the awnings tilt

Only you remain in your burnt umber
You stay in bed in the shadow of the palace lagging behind
as if you were killed in action
Only you stay behind like three houses, surviving

You stay in the shade of the tree or what
          remains of it
Ten minus eight leaves two—your eyes around me

ON BECOMING A PERSON

The night I decided to paradoxically intend
I had the wished-for bad dreams.
Elizabeth Bishop, whose "2000
Illustrations" this shows I had been reading
was whistling in a nightgown and playing and
singing to her family,
"I am the death tree,
I grow spontaneously,
I grow in the round,
Plant death in the ground"
after which duet
was played on the $59 Sony cassette
she became lugubrious, dramatic,
or conversely lubricated, and mellow,
and sighingly said,
Now I am going to bed, like a good girl!

In a sense, we are all child prodigies.
"I offer my frayed body to
            your corruscating soul
I open my used out eyes to your looming mouth
And my song which is yours in the
            old air of time
Big treaties on paper which fall from rock to rock"

A PROBLEM

There are two ways of living on the earth
Satisfied or dissatisfied. If satisfied,
Then leaving it for the stars will only make matters
        mathematically worse
If dissatisfied, then one will be dissatisfied with the stars.

One arrives in England, and the train station is a dirty toad.
Father takes a plane on credit card with medical telephone.
One calls up America at three-thirty, one's fiancée is morally
        alone.
But the patient is forever strapped to the seat in mild turbulence.

Thinking of America along psychoanalytic lines, and then
        delicately engraving nipples
On each of two round skulls
You have learned nothing from music but Debussy's ions
And the cover of the book is a forest with two lovers with empty
        cerebella.

Beyond the couple is a second girl, her head smeared out.
This represents early love, which is now "total space."
These are the ways of living on the earth,
Satisfied or unsatisfied. Snow keeps falling into the brook of
        wild rice.

A FAMILY SLIDE

Family on the slide, you should say!
See if this slide fits—
It rained yesterday; it rained today—
I told you we had duplicates

Oh no it's in backwards
It doesn't matter
Debbie's right that's the reverse
It doesn't matter

Is this my 16th birthday
All my fancy friends
Judy looks gorgeous but her friends
All look strange—slender and vital is a cliché

Who are these people now?
People you no longer know.
Who are these old women?
Are they young women?

Stupendous horrendous tremendous
And the fourth word is———hazardous!
Hazardous! hazardous! hunh! Everybody had a hint!
Just remember Mother had the same hint!

UNIVERSITY OF WINNIPEG
LIBRARY
DISCARDED
Winnipeg, Manitoba R3B 2E9

Is it a popular word, Walter, in everyday use?
It may not be in use everyday
But it COULD be in use everyday.
Momentous, bomentous . . .

Oh that's when we wanted Naomi to compete
In the Greenwood Pool contest
But she wanted nothing to do with it.
Good! "Why?" Why! We don't believe in a Beauty Contest!

("I believe in Beauty Contests.")
Who is this person?
That's you, and what's more that's me sitting behind you.
Know thyself, know thyself, is a famous expression.

Gnothi sauton, but who said it in English?
Pass the next slide please and don't ask who.
Don't worry about the viewer, the batteries are rechargeable.
Through photosynthesis, we're rechargeable too.

Once in a while Irv took a nice picture.
Like the one of Judy in Binghamton looking like a violin
And here is David playing on the shore
Mr. Eisenberg says, "Let me out and let the dog in"

Lao Tse said doing nothing was the way
To get along and little Debbie knows the dynasty
The bending reed won't break they say
But mother says, "If you bend it enough in the same place it
      may."

39

KASTALIE

A nude girl and boy embrace. Their heads are missing.
The movement is slightly
antithetic.
Mediocre work of the 20th century.
On the right, another nude doctor's boy.
For "analogies" read "characteristic features"

"You take a bath, but I drink it. Is that good. No it isn't."

The tensed leg
Above her in freedom the shroud
who holds a mask over the rt shoulder of Silenus
Between her legs her left hand
and on her right
Heavy but beautiful
for her breast is at the top
Behind her the sculpture of the balustrade
leaning slightly on her hand, tradition

Below, the inscription
Eros stands lightly
on the ledge "bent forward"   "adjacent"   "developed"
"advanced"
"Hello, good and happy one"
The glance, without direction
is a final effort.

40

FROM LOCUS SOLUS: AN OPERA
after R. Roussel

1. RICHARD WAGNER IN HIS MOTHER'S ARMS

This is my baby,
Richard Wagner,
Later to write
Die Götterdämmerung.

Now only five months,
Sleeping, a child
Inspiring charlatans
To make predictions.

Sleep, baby Richard,
In your mother's arms.
Later you will write
Die Götterdämmerung.

2. VOLTAIRE, RISING AND FALLING

Dubito dubito dubito
dubito dubito dubito
dubito dubito dubito

Dubito dubito dubito
Dubito dubito dubito
Dubito dubito dubito

3. MASTER CANTEREL

At first I was astonished by dancing insects
And the luminosity
Of impalpable clairvoyants. But now—

Now you know all the secrets of my park
Let's take the road back
Where a happy dinner will unite us all

Night is being made and the moon
Is almost round
It shines brilliantly in a cloudless sky

HANDAR

The hand not giving belongs to you
　　　but this is double (doubtful)
superceded eventually by many other hands
　　　and nearly steel-wooled out

　　　This was to be an illustration of my hand
　　　　　your hand X's hand
Rising from the storm out of the Atlantic
　　　while you held all the cards

But the cards seem to be dealt all at once
　　　in this uninhabitable world
　　Grasping, touching, retaining
those dense possessions that take their hold

spreading your finger-like beauties
　　　and bundles as in a children's game
we were living together as is said
　　　like the enemy ever at hand

　　　I was just painting you or grasping you
by accident by my spray-gun

And so the hand, ringing a small bell
　　　and no longer carrying the "basket of willows"
like the gorilla's hand is shorter, clumsier, heavier
　　　but it too crumbles beneath the spray of time

We too prisoners, as distinguished from one
handcuffed between distant goals

Now only adverbs
        mounting into a series with a sigh
carried along then like india-ink bottles
        punctured by the subway into prayer

                I was just painting your hand
        solemn form, now knitting up

Come, deaf and dumb, carrying your portable
        firearms

The storm has grown up by hand
You try to control spray-guns at very close intervals—

It's almost impossible to do

What was awful was that
The love poem ended with a wild rat

In your hand I saw the giant word RED painted in green

The storm has grown up by hand
        littering all our mirrors all our specimens
but some birds have been bandaged by the attendants
        for the benefit of air

FATHER KNOWS BEST

It is the old show, but the young son can fly.
He sees pink and blue and red umbrellas in the air.
They teach him how to fly.
Of course the family does not see and has resentments.

One day at a snow party he tries to prove he can fly.
But he only leaps a bit and loses the jumping contest.
Then Father realizes son must enclose but a few electrons
                    of air in his fist
Then son flies high above the family garage and trees,
                    branch by branch.

There are no umbrellas, there are only frosty parachutes,
Little angels who instruct him how to fly.
He must not struggle too much with his hands,
Which having practised the violin now dog-paddle in air.

High above the invigorated gulf the air walks down its
                    own road.
And sister jumps up in a dual column of wind.
Inside, Mother serves breakfast; the bluejay gulps at
                    the feeding-station.
The family now knows he can fly, but still father knows best.

R's DILEMMA

"If I like Solomon
Could have my dream
My dream
To write down almost all the dreams I've ever had
Since that first one aged five
In which I'm slipping up on sand
While a pistol
Is just out of view
Till the one I had in Crete
That opened up
Into five dreams
In which I am flying and others in the dream
Are misinterpreting due to "The Interpretation of Dreams"
Something about the only organ that defies gravity
I don't correct them, just go on flying
Under the trees
This dream-diary of mine
Would be more than a poem
A whole *paysage* with burnt umber leaves
And no rake
But unfortunately, I don't have the stamina to do it
I'm lucky to have gotten this down."

VIEW

When I was asleep you beat me
Happy in the laxity of night.
As Sophocles and Niobe cried out
Inert day put out its precursor's small quantity of light.

When we were mascot scouts like little leaves
Grandma propped on the sand like President Lincoln
The blimps paused above us with their tiny brakes
Last threads that held us to the sky!

I thought of you as frangible as badly broken reefs
Where Darwin's spirit sleeps and cannot wake any longer,
To observe this moth on the ceiling screaming with remorse:
Then his blue wisdom would be effaced; the Voyage of the
          Beagle without eyes.

Tonight the floor is full of fancy flowers from old brains
And a grainy aplomb as at the end of the world.
All tightness is slowed down and dipped into
          compromised ideas.
Golden uncertainty has given you time to decide.

CASCADE

"Notre vie coule de roche en roche"

—*Reverdy*

I left my dilatory feet in the golden sand.
Nothing in normal light but a summer broken off:
You can still see the entire foot from the broken piece.
Alone and vague it hesitates to mount the boards.

The tree, encircled by vague moss, is inflated as if by disdain.
Not a word glides by that does not lose itself among cinders.
You laughed, your eyes lowered like the fire itself.
Finally it was necessary to go lower than your forehead: a
        curtain.

Surely the source of so much blood must be an event, if not
        blessing.
The axe among flowers is getting longer and longer:
Now it is two axes, carving out a portico as the sky burgeons
        and flees.
Then you lower all the eyelids, and we breathe together a long
        time.

It is always the same, the same foot stuck in the forest,
As one stumbles, the same bottles balanced on trees,
Craning your neck to look without pity at this rigamarole,
Character traits of our life, which runs from rock to rock.

ABOUT THIS COURSE

The leaf twists and turns, then floats down the drain.
Surely in all nature there's no motion more ordinary.
And even if we were to describe it, what would we gain?

Each leaf would seem to require its own quatrain.
Indeed, this is typical of most earth events' individuality.
The leaf twists and turns, then floats down the drain.

And so, facing this dilemma, like the scatterbrain
We are, at least for a little while, we leave the leaf laboratory
And even if we were to describe it, what would we gain?

We want to describe motion, but the motions are insane
Typical of most earth events occurring simultaneously.
The leaf twists and turns, then floats down the drain.

The leaf like you in rain looks almost human—
Powerless, almost comfortable, as predicted by theory,
And even if we were to describe it, what would we gain?

You too seem to rot quietly on the proverbial vine
But like rifle bullets you vibrate incessantly.
The leaf twists and turns, then floats down the drain.
And even if we were to describe it, what would we gain?

That morning that we rolled our undisturbed
        path

Made clear what was really important: straight out
        into space
The balloon jumped forward and a little air spurt
        out
In the opposite direction: Our tug-of-war took us,
        two observers
You to the barge, I to the drifting shore: we each
        gave our report of the incident:
An apple and a kite and a negligible feather kept
        falling,
A man kept running into his tent; the field (which,
        sagging slightly, had been pushing up on your body)
Suddenly gave way—you hardly felt me falling beside
        you
But this does not mean I had lost my weight which could
        only happen if the earth were removed
Or shook back and forth sideways in far, interstellar
        space.

Weren't you surprised? You watched the
        frictionless device
And smoothly it glided along as after your
        slightest nudge.
It showed no sign of failing our everyday
        elation.
Yet it was behaving quite as naturally as
        a table.
Then you took off and glided across
        the floor,
Just like a dry-ice disk, as it challenges
        our notion of the natural.
The bluejay kept a moving worm from
        moving forever.
Of course the violin did not fall to the ground
        as soon as I lost contact with the bowstring.

But the sensation was of lying on a soft bed of sound.
　　Weren't you surprised? "One beat of a fly's wing,
One pulse of a laser, the time between heartbeats,
　　a strobe-flash duration"—The question is fair enough, but
　　there is no answer.

The flame goes up and the smoke keeps travelling
　　down;
The sun is in the zenith and the watery sap flows so
　　abundantly from a cut branch: in a short time
It fills a glass and forms a cool
　　refreshing beverage;
The flame goes up and the smoke keeps travelling
　　down;
Actually a photo of you is being pushed across the sky,
　　as if to fix everything;
Nevertheless one must get started on one's work and
　　overcome by storm the shadows: it blows against us
And so the cars and pucks, that skid along, since the
　　table or road is attached to the earth,
Are skidding toward the heat death of their
　　world;
The entire earth is but a baseball thrown horizontally,
　　our hands crumple up or smash up or dent
Or stick together and heat up and have their insides
　　changed;
And we, like the water at the bottom of the waterfall, awake in
　　anechoic chambers

I filled a swimming pool with chairs, and all
　　who swim must dive between:
My father's viola, my sister's cello, my
　　sister's violin,

My uncle's piano, my mother's piano, my sister's
        cello,
My father's violin, my sister's cello,
        my grandfather's voice.
I am not a meteorologist. I am a poet. Why? Well, in the
        fall the cricket is a better reader of heat than most.
Listen to a cricket for fourteen seconds; add forty; and that's
        the heat, that's how hot it is where the cricket is.
Now if the cricket sang 34 times in fourteen—sang how hot
        it is—how hot would that be?
Not too hot. Now I want to start my song "My butterfly,
        my bee."
Bufo americanus, throat of male, loose and dark, it may be
        heard of rainy nights

The first time we see we are standing in a
        windowless elevator
The elevator is falling through its shaft, falling,
        falling.
We keep dropping coins from our pockets to the floor,
        but the coins float away.
Then we throw our pens against the wall, but those pens
        never reach the wall.
We conclude we are in outer space, because there is no gravity.
But we are only standing in an elevator, falling,
        falling.
The second time we see we are in the same elevator,
        in the middle of outer space,
Drawn by a long cable, attached to some supernatural
        force, consistently accelerating,
We keep dropping our coins and throw our pens forward again—
        this time everything lands with a splat
We conclude we are only in an elevator falling through its shaft,
        but our legs feel heavy—we are really in space: the earth
            a pencil-dot.

Well-known largely because of my inability to fly, I have
    gained a place in the literature if not your backyard.
I have no noticeable wings or tails and since I am flightless
    I live on the ground.
We are related, but even this relationship is not close
    enough.
In a hole I am well-hidden. When young I closely resembled
    the adult.
Now that I am old I can run. Others can fly away, but require
    considerable area to get a running start.
But for you flight is easy. And you are more slender than
    these. "The ground dove nests on ground or in the trees."
We ourselves are fastened to opposite ends, your head
    adjustable from the outside
Carries a mirror so that it is kept steady: in this case I
    am exhausted, detecting a grain
Of repulsion: the pressure of two lamp-blackened
    lovers: the faces more heated than bright
Then the faces recede, as though repelled by light
    bodies, but this explanation is inadequate.

They treat us like dirt, and we are dirt too
    turning black at maturity with the skin stretched,
Like a somewhat tight glove which is forced upon the hand
    on the diamond, quantities of children running home,
But powerless to exempt themselves from falling clay,
    and from falling bats,
Consenting to this on their knees, the rudimentary
    club,
Lowered down as part of the weather uh . . .
    probably
Few persons escape, though it may remain very localized, like
    fingernail polish,
Those half-human features magnified: eyes at the top, ears at
    the side, and the mouth is lower down,

And as stars fall unproductively into the lake, no bigger
      than a woman's hand among cloven feet,
A rather attractive hand when opening among clouds, with
      chances to recover you in one piece, on the way to bat.
The eyes are vestigial. The nose is an ornament. And we will
      neither grow old nor look old.

Here, their passports are taken away from them.
      On the ship, there is an international airport.
The sperm whales float along, waiting their turn
      to be taken to the factory,
Verdicts are executed to the accompaniment of
      music, the boat is slow because it travels through
          restrictions,
Injured people confess they were born without arteries, and are
      arrested in hospital on grounds of carelessly causing death,
Ultrasonic impulses keep them crimped to a group. In exchange
      for a spic and span lunch which they enjoy
All the way downstream, taking advantage of
      the loopholes,
They are given a numbered ticket which allows them to land, at
      a duty-free shop to visit the folks for three hours,
But even while they wait they are marked with
      Roman numerals
They have used the bodies of children as improvised bridges,
      which they later cross.

In school they teach you about osmosis but not why things
      stick together
And they stick together because nothing else is between
      them.
We adhere because we are so close, and only because of
      that.
The stars go thoroughly into the sky. The youthful murderer
      is identified by his mother.

The gun is recovered from the interior of the
    television set
The pinpricks are so close together one feels only the one
    solitary pinprick.
And as the whale's stomach is split open, its last
    meal is revealed.
"I couldn't draw my mind but this was on my mind
    It was a horse maybe—it was you and me—
It was dirt—plunk—it was a sparkling round sleep-
    inducing diamond, from which thoughts
Departed according to their sizes. It was a horse
    of many holes, you see."
The hens lay eggs under the artificial light, believing
    that day has come.

The months had almost put a soft pedal on the mouth,
    but presently showing the cymbals' inner sides, in triumph
After clashing them, it might sound more like kerbang!
    or powie! It's the dead sound I'm trying to apply . . .
You like the agreement of sounds all right, but its history
    has been pretty resolutely purred or yapped out,
With my toot between your teeth and midday smelling of
    English kisses, *silentium altum* put the gag on you
A drum-head and drum-skin and a drum-stick already seen
    to split attention like a conch.
You are the prime work of God and you smell like a scent-bag!
    So listen to the songish program
In which I am the sparrow and you the itinerant gleemaiden
    or streetsinger carrying sheet music up the smeared street.
And the music rolls past you as trees are tied up together
    and the past repeated by arrangement with the Conductor
And it is crying, to you, like a hurrah of tigers, in full possession
    of their faculties, unexaggerated animals, because weeping
        without

Reservation, by my troth, puffing and hot, as a confused ship is
      intimidated by the land which turns out to be compassionate.

The earth being both a lodestone and a
      baseball
Light bounces off the mirror. Light
      persists
But has to be given up in the long run, like
      little balls, as far too limited
We have lived by the light of this empty
      space,
This information of canvasses painted by
      beams,
Not by masters, unappreciated light because not
      easily separated from hide and go seek.
You played a truncated version, covering your
      eyes
Thinking that you could never be seen, as I see you
      now.
And we are skidding like a bullet in a
      tree stump
Entering at top speed but coming to rest like two pennies,
      one on top of the other.

The finest pencil one can imagine is just
      a shadow
A ray of light is something they invented to shoot
      bullets through without causing it to flicker
You can pass your hand right through the bulb
      without feeling a thing
It's the little lamp that isn't there, like the kilogram
      that carefully protected cylinder at Sèvres
With a bug on it, though I hate to say it, light
      which even if it doesn't fall at 45° is nonetheless light

Each clear evening discovering dozens if not
      hundreds of new stars
But we concentrate ourselves further on smaller and
      smaller mirrors
And eventually the mirrors are as small as a single false note
      interrupting a tiny dead day
What is light? Watch your feet, my data lie
      underneath them.
What is light? It is something different from all
      that we have studied.

We have been sailing in a certain small fountain,
      like physicists in toy boats
Each craft bears a candle on its deck. We light the
      candles and the boats puff by
As if you were real, delightful. And we who have never
      been able to resist
The course of a new toy dream have spent much time
      watching the fun in the fountains.
And if we, in a sense, sink in that water,
      the goldfish, I am sure, will retain
Their silver dignity. We are fed beside the
      fountains
As the young are fed by the experiment and the
      results.
It confirms us; and now the whole water
      is silver;
A crucial step is taken, but years
      later,
The fountain is slowed down, as if controlled
      by your calm hands.

DAVID SHAPIRO teaches in the English
Department at Columbia College. He was
born in Newark, N.J., in 1947 and has
degrees from both Columbia and Cambridge
University. His poems have appeared
in many magazines, and journals, including
Poetry (Chicago), *Paris Review*, and *The New Yorker*.
He was the recipient of a Merrill Foundation
grant, a Robert Frost Fellowship at Breadloaf,
and the Book-of-the-Month Club Award, as
well as a Kellet Fellowship to Clare College,
Cambridge. Since 1964 he has taught children
for The Academy of American Poets, the
Bedford-Stuyvesant Children's Museum, Lincoln
Center, and Teachers and Writers Collaborative.
His art criticism has appeared in *Art News*
and *Craft Horizons*.
His last book, *A Man Holding an Acoustic Panel*,
was nominated for a National Book Award in 1972.